Fly a life-size **HICCUP** and **TOOTHLESS**!

Try your hand at training **STORMFLY**!

Make **MEATLUG** fly forwards, backwards and hover!

Explore the app to discover more facts and stats about the dragons!

D0274882

This is a Carlton Book
Text and design Carlton Books Limited 2017

DreamWorks Dragons © 2017 DreamWorks
Animation LLC. All Rights Reserved.

First published in the UK in 2017
by Carlton Books Limited
20 Mortimer Street, London W1T 3JW

A catalogue record for this book is
available from the British Library.

ISBN: 978-1-78312-301-8
1 3 5 7 9 10 8 6 4 2
Printed in Dongguan, China

Author: Emily Stead
Executive Editor: Jo Casey
Designer: Darren Jordan
Junior Designer: Kate Wiliwinska
Digital Producer: Sean Daly
Production Controller: Yael Steinitz

CARLTON
KiDS

DRAGONS
...ME TO LIFE!

WELCOME TO BERK...

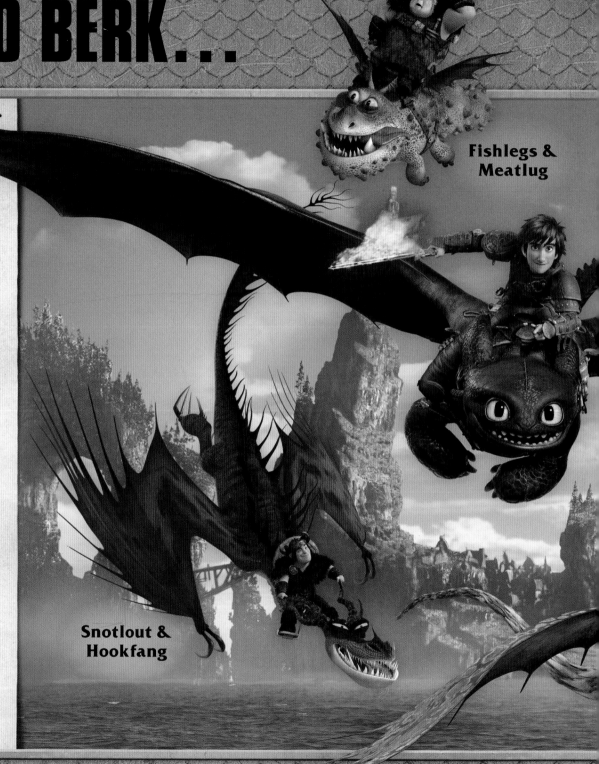

... an island where it snows nine months of the year, and hails the other three. Any food that grows here is tough and tasteless. The people that grow here are even more so. The only upsides are the pets. While other places have ponies or parrots, Berk has... dragons.

Dragons used to be a problem on Berk until the day when Hiccup, son of a Viking chief, made friends with a fearsome Night Fury dragon, and life on the island changed forever.

Now, times are peaceful on the island, and the Vikings of Berk and dragons live side by side. The humans and their one-time foes continue to learn about each other with each day that passes. Read on to discover all about the wildest, most dangerous creatures on Earth and those who tamed them...

Fishlegs & Meatlug

Snotlout & Hookfang

**Ruffnut & Tuffnut
and Barf & Belch**

**Hiccup &
Toothless**

**Astrid &
Stormfly**

An unlikely friendship was formed when Hiccup knocked down a Night Fury.

After Hiccup trained Toothless, other species of dragons were tamed, too.

Dragons had previously been the Vikings' deadly enemies for centuries.

7

One of the cleverest of all dragon species, Toothless is a feared Night Fury. He is thought to be the last of his kind. Jet-black scales cover his whole body and allow him to fly at night without being seen. This loyal dragon is smart, fast and best friends with Hiccup.

FLY A NIGHT FURY
Fly a life-size Toothless and Hiccup around your local park!

Night Fury Facts

🌿 Hiccup created a new left tailfin for Toothless after the dragon's real one was injured in a crash. Now Toothless can fly again but only with his rider, Hiccup, controlling the tailfin with an ingenious saddle Hiccup invented and built.

🌿 Toothless's bravest moment was when he plunged hundreds of metres on his own to save Hiccup from crashing to the ground after the epic battle with the Red Death.

🌿 Toothless is not actually toothless, but he does have retractable teeth that sometimes make him look that way.

🌿 Hiccup's mum, Valka, revealed a row of hidden spikes on Toothless's back that help him to fly even faster.

Special Species
Toothless has a special ability – echolocation – that is a bit like radar. When his sight is limited, such as in a pitch-black cave, he can emit a sound wave, which bounces off nearby terrain and obstacles, telling Toothless exactly what's around him.

Meet Hiccup, expert Dragon Rider and current chief of Berk. He's the son of Stoick the Vast and Valka. Hiccup discovered how to train dragons and, as a result, he brought peace between dragons and the Vikings of Berk.

Miserable Meeting

Toothless and Hiccup make a terrific team, but they weren't always on the same side. The pair first met when Hiccup brought down Toothless from the sky with another ingenious invention, the Mangler, during a provisions raid of the Vikings' village by scores of dragons. Now they share an unbreakable bond and hate to be apart.

DRAGON STATS

ATTACK	15	SHOT LIMIT	6
SPEED	20	VENOM	0
ARMOUR	18	JAW STRENGTH	6
FIREPOWER	14	STEALTH	18

The Night Fury is the fastest, smartest and rarest of the known dragon species.

STORMFLY

This blue and yellow dragon is as deadly as she is beautiful. She preens and grooms herself like a peacock, and will stop and admire her reflection when passing a mirror-like surface. Don't let her good looks fool you, though! One of the speediest in the skies, Stormfly is hard to beat in a Dragon Race.

TRAIN A TRACKER
Try your hand at helping Stormfly take flight!

Pretty Deadly
Deadly Nadder Stormfly may look pretty, but she is deadly in battle. She can shoot poisonous spines from her tail – a powerful secret weapon.

Deadly Nadder Facts
⊕ Astrid has taught Stormfly how to fetch like a dog.

⊕ Her favourite treat to eat is chicken.

⊕ Stormfly is part of the Tracker Class of dragons because of her incredible sense of smell and ability to track a human or dragon. She can sniff out an enemy from 30 metres away.

⊕ She has a blind spot in front of her nose.

ASTRID

Astrid is Stormfly's human rider and best friend. When Astrid wakes up each morning, Stormfly's head pokes through the shutters to greet her! Just like her dragon, Astrid is tough and beautiful, and would stop at nothing to defend the ones she loves.

Stormy Start

Rider Astrid and Stormfly weren't always so close – when they first met in dragon training (before the Vikings and dragons became friends), Astrid hit Stormfly in the face to save herself from Stormfly's attack! These days they don't like to be separated and care about each other very much. Stormfly is loyal to Astrid and doesn't invite other trainers to ride her.

DRAGON STATS

ATTACK	10	SHOT LIMIT	6
SPEED	8	VENOM	16
ARMOUR	16	JAW STRENGTH	5
FIREPOWER	18	STEALTH	10

Deadly Nadders have blind spots in front of their noses, so it's safest to stand in front of them!

BEYOND BERK

On their adventures on and beyond the Isle of Berk, Hiccup and his friends have discovered many rare and beautiful dragons. Hiccup has recorded the location of each dragon species on a map he drew himself.

Dragon Island

Dragon Island remained undiscovered for centuries as it is usually shrouded in fog. Once home to the fearsome dragon the Red Death during its reign of terror, the island is now the tyrant's final resting place.

Raven Point

This wooded mountaintop is where Hiccup and Toothless first met. No one could have predicted that the encounter would change the relationship between Vikings and dragons forever.

The Rookery

Dragons flock to this warm haven every winter to welcome their new hatchlings and teach them to fly.

Dragon's Edge
Beyond Berk and away from the archipelago, Dragon's Edge is a base for the Dragon Riders, and the departure point for their journeys to far-off new lands with unfamiliar adversaries.

Horrendous Point
Hiccup's family is so famous on Berk that they even have a mountain named after them! Legend has it that any Viking who falls asleep on this tall peak will dream of their future.

Badmist Mountains
This mountain range at the northern edge of Berk is one of Toothless's top spots. You'll most likely find the Night Fury hanging out here if Hiccup isn't riding him.

Isle of Berk
Berk is a small island with rocky outcrops, beaches, waterfalls, streams and several large forests. If it wasn't so freezing and grey, it would be quite pretty. Once the Vikings' enemies, dragons are now welcomed here.

Island of Night
While no Night Furies are known to live here, the isle gets its name from the dark rocks and tall cliffs that keep it veiled in darkness night or day.

MEATLUG

Meatlug is loving and affectionate to her Dragon Rider, Fishlegs. The pair do everything together, from flying to relaxing and hanging out together. Meatlug also accompanies Fishlegs when he researches dragon trivia.

Gentle Dragons

Gronckles may look menacing, but they are a gentle dragon species. They have small, squat bodies and oversized heads. Their fire blast is devastating – a Gronckle chews rocks, then spews them out as balls of molten lava.

FLYING LESSON
Make Meatlug fly forwards, backwards and hover!

Gronckle Facts

 Gronckles can be lazy and spend a lot of time napping. They sometimes even fall asleep while flying, often waking up having splashed into the ocean or crashed into the side of a mountain!

 Gronckles are the only dragons known to fly forwards, backwards and sideways – and they can even hover thanks to their compact, fast-fluttering wings.

 A Gronckle can't produce fire if its head is wet.

 Baby Gronckles don't hatch from eggs like other dragon species; they explode out of their shells!

FISHLEGS

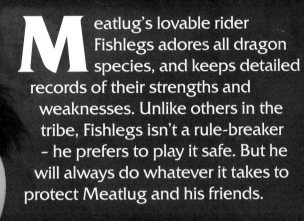

Meatlug's lovable rider Fishlegs adores all dragon species, and keeps detailed records of their strengths and weaknesses. Unlike others in the tribe, Fishlegs isn't a rule-breaker – he prefers to play it safe. But he will always do whatever it takes to protect Meatlug and his friends.

DRAGON STATS

ATTACK	8	SHOT LIMIT	6
SPEED	4	VENOM	0
ARMOUR	20	JAW STRENGTH	8
FIREPOWER	14	STEALTH	5

Meatlug is sweet and affectionate – just like her rider, Fishlegs!

Perfect Pairing
Fishlegs and Meatlug really are the perfect pair. Meatlug likes to lick Fishlegs's feet before they go to sleep and Fishlegs often makes up songs about Meatlug and calls her 'Princess Meatlug'.

A powerful fire-breather, the Monstrous Nightmare Hookfang is huge. While most dragons obey their riders, disobedient Hookfang often chooses to do the opposite of what Snotlout tells him! Despite Hookfang not listening to Snotlout, they are both warriors at heart.

◉ This dragon species truly is the stuff of nightmares! It's enormous, arrogant and does exactly as it likes.

◉ Kerosene seeps from the skin of a Monstrous Nightmare, so when the dragon breathes fire, its skin sets alight, too. No damage is done to the dragon, but it's a frightening sight for its enemy.

◉ Hookfang has an incredible wingspan of more than 20 metres.

◉ Hookfang's horns lack extra antlers, which helps Snotlout to tell him apart from other Monstrous Nightmares.

Dragon Training

At first, Snotlout was wary of dragons. He would rather strike first and ask questions later. But with Hiccup's help, Snotlout managed to make friends with Hookfang and become his rider. Now they make a tremendous team, either in combat or in competition with the other Dragon Riders.

Bullheaded Snotlout is Hookfang's rider. Snotlout's main gift is his strength – he is often seen carrying sheep above his head – which goes a little way to make up for his brutish behaviour. Stubborn and arrogant, Snotlout is not unlike his dragon. Although Hookfang almost never follows Snotlout's commands, the pair do care for one another.

DRAGON STATS

ATTACK	15	SHOT LIMIT	10
SPEED	16	VENOM	0
ARMOUR	12	JAW STRENGTH	6
FIREPOWER	15	STEALTH	9

If under threat, the Monstrous Nightmare will coat itself with fire from nose to tail.

NIGHTMARE IN FLIGHT
Dare you take control of the fiery Hookfang?

BARF & BELCH

Barf & Belch belong to the Hideous Zippleback species, an unusual and dangerous type of dragon. Just like the twins that ride them, Barf & Belch spend more time bickering than working together, proving that two heads are not always better than one. They are strong and agile, but can get their necks in a tangle at times.

Hideous Zippleback Facts

🐉 This unusual dragon has two long, spiked serpentine necks. The spikes can lock together and create the illusion of one neck.

🐉 Zipplebacks can fly, but their small wings keep these dragons grounded most of the time.

🐉 Instead of breathing fire, one head breathes a thick green gas, then the other head ignites it – an explosive combination!

TRAIN TWO HEADS
Watch Barf & Belch rear up their heads before your eyes!

RUFFNUT & TUFFNUT

Twins Ruffnut & Tuffnut are a danger-loving duo. They share a passion for taking risks – no challenge is too deadly for Ruff & Tuff! Sister Ruff has a snarky manner and a foul temper, while her brother Tuff is fearless and daring.

Twin Riders

When Ruffnut & Tuffnut took charge of Barf & Belch, they used to shout instructions to their dragons at the same time. The result was chaos! These days the riders and dragons work as a team (most of the time).

DRAGON STATS

ATTACK	12	SHOT LIMIT	6
SPEED	10	VENOM	0
ARMOUR	10	JAW STRENGTH	6 (3X2)
FIREPOWER	14	STEALTH	22 (11X2)

Barf & Belch spend a lot of their time bickering, but occasionally they do get along.

WINDSHEAR

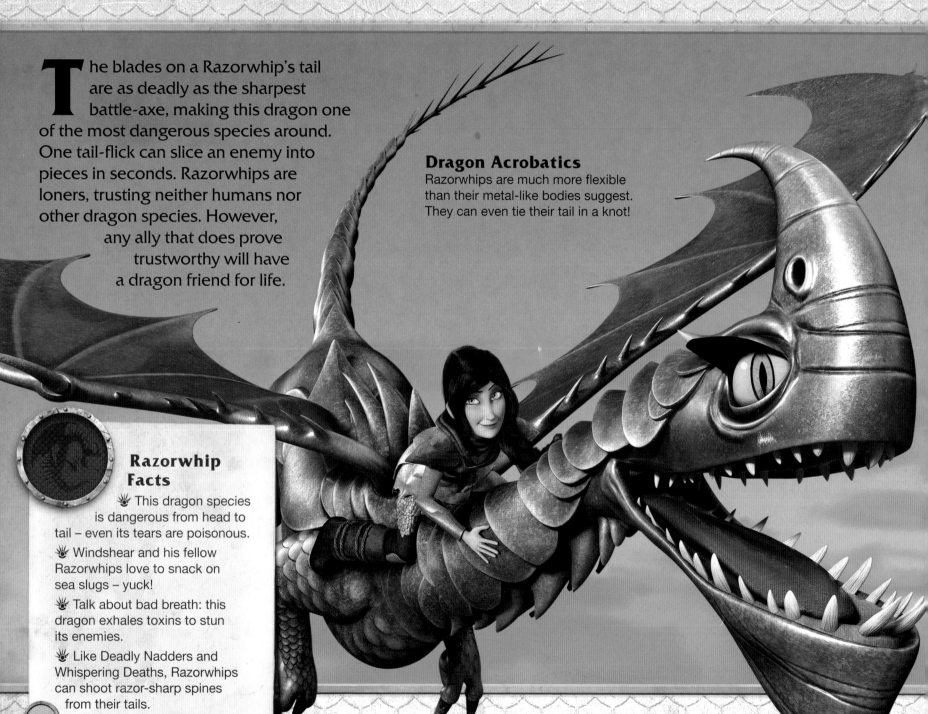

The blades on a Razorwhip's tail are as deadly as the sharpest battle-axe, making this dragon one of the most dangerous species around. One tail-flick can slice an enemy into pieces in seconds. Razorwhips are loners, trusting neither humans nor other dragon species. However, any ally that does prove trustworthy will have a dragon friend for life.

Dragon Acrobatics
Razorwhips are much more flexible than their metal-like bodies suggest. They can even tie their tail in a knot!

Razorwhip Facts

🐾 This dragon species is dangerous from head to tail – even its tears are poisonous.

🐾 Windshear and his fellow Razorwhips love to snack on sea slugs – yuck!

🐾 Talk about bad breath: this dragon exhales toxins to stun its enemies.

🐾 Like Deadly Nadders and Whispering Deaths, Razorwhips can shoot razor-sharp spines from their tails.

HEATHER

Heather and Windshear share an unbreakable bond, having both known tragedy. Together, they raid pirate ships and return the stolen goods to their rightful owners. Heather's relationship with the other Dragon Riders has been rocky. She has proved to be untrustworthy more than once, and is known as the Rogue Dragon Rider.

Healing Wounds

While Windshear appears unfriendly to other Dragon Riders, she is extremely close to Heather. She trained Windshear after nursing the dragon back to health following a Typhoomerang attack. The pair then formed a perfect partnership.

DRAGON STATS

ATTACK	18	SHOT LIMIT	10
SPEED	18	VENOM	8
ARMOUR	32	JAW STRENGTH	7
FIREPOWER	12	STEALTH	5

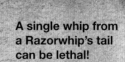

A single whip from a Razorwhip's tail can be lethal!

SKULLCRUSHER

Skullcrusher was the first of the Rumblehorn species of dragons to be discovered by the Vikings. These Tracker Class dragons can sniff out targets from the faintest of scents – they are the dragon version of a bloodhound! Skullcrusher tracked down Hiccup in Valka's nest with Hiccup's lost helmet the only clue.

Rumblehorn Facts

☀ The rough Rumblehorn has a rhino-like head, which it uses as a battering ram.

☀ A Rumblehorn's secret weapon is its ability to launch long-range fiery missile-like blasts.

☀ Stoick named his Rumblehorn 'Skullcrusher', as they both have heads as hard as iron.

☀ Skullcrusher became Stoick's dragon after he released Thornado to raise some infant Thunderdrums.

Headstrong Hero

Skullcrusher once tried to warn the Dragon Riders that a tidal wave was on its way, but the only Viking who believed him was Stoick. With Skullcrusher's help, Stoick and the riders were able to save the outpost, just in time.

STOICK

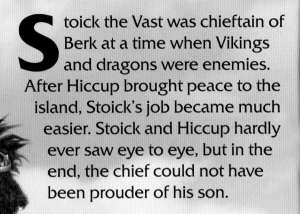

S toick the Vast was chieftain of Berk at a time when Vikings and dragons were enemies. After Hiccup brought peace to the island, Stoick's job became much easier. Stoick and Hiccup hardly ever saw eye to eye, but in the end, the chief could not have been prouder of his son.

Legend

Stoick died in an accident when Toothless was tricked into attacking him. A mountain of a man, Stoick will remain in Viking legend forever.

Stoick was overjoyed to be reunited with his wife Valka after so many years apart.

DRAGON STATS

ATTACK	12	SHOT LIMIT	4
SPEED	4	VENOM	0
ARMOUR	10	JAW STRENGTH	5
FIREPOWER	13		

Following the death of Stoick, Skullcrusher found a new rider in Eret.

GRUMP

Grump belongs to a breed of Boulder Class dragons known as Hotburple. Its body is covered in copper and grey scales, and its ears and teeth look similar to a Gronckle. While Gronckles eat boulders to create their lava blasts, Hotburples shoot flaming chunks of lava.

Hotburple Facts

⚙ Hotburples eat a diet of scraps of iron, which they use to make slugs of molten lava.

⚙ Like Gronckles, Hotburples are lazy layabouts. Their snores are so loud, they echo for miles around.

⚙ The Hotburple's wingspan is much bigger than a Gronckle's, and the bludgeon on its tail is rounder and bulbous.

⚙ Of all the dragon species, the Hotburple is the only one strong enough to bite through dragon-proof bars.

Lazy but Loyal

Grump is extremely lazy – when he's not sleeping he is usually eating! Grump is loyal to his rider Gobber and would do anything to help him.

GOBBER

A trusted friend of Stoick, Gobber is also the blacksmith on Berk. He used to forge weapons for battles with dragons, but these days he spends his time building saddles to ride them and even performs dragon dentistry!

Loyal Servant

Steadfast Gobber is incredibly loyal and is always willing to help his Viking clan. He is a great mentor with a huge heart and would do anything for anyone – he just doesn't want anyone to know it!

DRAGON STATS

ATTACK	8	SHOT LIMIT	6
SPEED	4	VENOM	0
ARMOUR	20	JAW STRENGTH	8
FIREPOWER	14	STEALTH	5

Gobber is known on Berk for his bravery, having lost his right hand and left leg to a Monstrous Nightmare.

Gobber and Stoick are the best of friends and always support each other.

FEARSOME FOES

W ith dragons no longer the enemy, a host of human villains now pose the biggest threat to the people of Berk. Anyone who treats dragons badly, keeps them prisoner or tries to trade the beautiful creatures becomes an instant adversary to Hiccup and his tribe. Read on to meet some of their fearsome foes.

DAGUR

Dagur the Deranged used to lead the Berserkers at a time when he was obsessed with plotting to hunt and capture Toothless. Once Hiccup's arch-enemy, Dagur switched sides and now rides dragons with the Hairy Hooligans.

Sly Skills

* Dagur used to take pleasure in slaying dragons, but now he cares for his own creature – a Gronckle called Shattermaster.

* He was imprisoned on Outcast Island for three years after being defeated by the Hooligans.

* Dagur's little sister is revealed to be Heather, who was separated from her family when she was young.

* His weapon of choice is an axe or a crossbow.

Hiccup holds the ancient Dragon Eye, a treasure that allows the Dragon Riders to discover new lands and new dragons.

RYKER

A menacing man, riches and wealth are what motivate the elder Grimborn brother, Ryker. He will oppose anyone who gets in his way, human or dragon. Ryker rarely speaks, but simply takes what he wants and discards it like an old dragon skin. The only person he cares for is his brother, Viggo.

Sly Skills

❋ Strong swordsmanship – Ryker can fight expertly with two swords.

❋ This hunter can sniff out dragon species by their smell alone.

❋ He is an excellent dragon-trapper and understands dragons' strengths and weaknesses.

❋ His archery skills make him a fearsome opponent.

VIGGO

If you thought Ryker was evil, you've never met his younger brother, Viggo. While Ryker has muscle and brawn, Viggo was the smart and ruthless one. He was the chief of the Dragon Hunters, whose main quest was to obtain the Dragon Eye to wipe out all dragons for profit. Viggo is believed to have died when a volcano erupted.

Sly Skills

❋ Viggo's knowledge of dragons equalled, if not outstripped, Hiccup's.

❋ He was an expert at playing the game Maces and Talons.

❋ Although he wasn't as strong as his brother, Ryker, Viggo possessed excellent combat skills.

Living side by side with dragons has taught Hiccup and the Vikings far more about these dynamic dragons than is revealed in Bork the Bold's *Book of Dragons*. Every dragon is different, but equally fascinating. These four dragons are just a few of the amazing species known to the Dragon Riders.

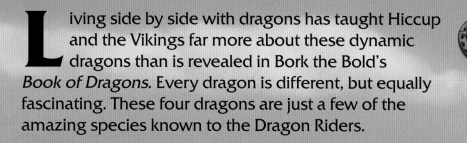

THUNDERDRUM

This sea dragon doesn't need to breathe fire to terrify – the sonic boom it creates in its enormous mouth is so strong it can wipe out an opponent from close range. The dragon likes to skim the surface of the ocean, ready to dive beneath the waves and swallow up a whole school of fish in one swoop. Stoick once rode a Thunderdrum called Thornado.

ATTACK	12	SHOT LIMIT	6
SPEED	14	VENOM	0
ARMOUR	10	JAW STRENGTH	7
FIREPOWER	16	STEALTH	8

STORMCUTTER

Valka's dragon is a sturdy Stormcutter called Cloudjumper, with fins that sprout from his face and tail. A second set of wings are revealed to allow the dragon to fly in an X formation and make tight turns. The sharp, hooked pincers at the talons of its wings are nimble enough to pick the lock of a dragon trap, yet strong enough to tear an enemy to shreds.

ATTACK	12	SHOT LIMIT	6
SPEED	14	VENOM	0
ARMOUR	10	JAW STRENGTH	7
FIREPOWER	16	STEALTH	8

SKRILL

A mysterious and unpredictable dragon, training a Skrill is almost impossible. Rather than breathe fire, this species channels lightning down its metallic spines to blast at opponents, or stores it to be released later. The Skrill can hibernate in icy glaciers for decades at a time, only to reappear as dangerous as the day it was frozen.

ATTACK	14	SHOT LIMIT	4
SPEED	11/19*	VENOM	0
ARMOUR	10	JAW STRENGTH	5
FIREPOWER	12	STEALTH	18

*with lightning

TIMBERJACK

Timberjacks are a sensitive species that like to spend their time in the forests they call home. Try not to fall out with one – a Timberjack's razor-sharp wings can slice through tree trunks and cause major destruction. When not used to attack, these huge wings can also act as a tent, offering shelter to Dragon Riders.

ATTACK	10	SHOT LIMIT	8
SPEED	12	VENOM	0
ARMOUR	8	JAW STRENGTH	3
FIREPOWER	10	STEALTH	13

TRAINER QUIZ

How would you fare in the field as a Dragon Rider? Are you a top trainer, like Hiccup and Dagur, or more of a dragon dunce? Try these tricky trainer quiz questions, then work out your score.

1. Which dragon can deliver a deafening sonic boom blast?

2. Which dragon became Hiccup's hero when he saved him from the Red Death?

3. Which fire-breather can tie its own tail in a knot?

4. Name the species whose attack method is to chew rocks and release them as molten lava.

5. Which baby dragon species explodes out of its shell at birth?

6. Which dragon's armour is the toughest?

7. Which dragon type does this symbol represent?

8. Look closely to discover the only dragon that has no legs.

9. Which dragon species' favourite food is a slurp of slimy sea slugs?

10. Look back through the book to find the speediest dragon.

11. Name three species that can shoot razor-sharp spines from their tails.

12. Which dragon species does not breathe fire?

Answers

1. Thunderdrum, 2. Toothless, 3. Razorwhip, 4. Gronckle, 5. Gronckle, 6. Windshear (Razorwhip), 7. Sharp Class, 8. Timberjack, 9. Razorwhip, 10. Toothless, 11. Deadly Nadders, Whispering Deaths, Razorwhips, 12. Skrill.